mouse and mongoose Find a Rainbow in Hawaiʻi

illustrated by Elizabeth Oh

BeachHouse

One morning, Mongoose knocked on Mouse's door. When Mouse answered, Mongoose said, "Aloha, Mouse. Will you help me find a rainbow? I have never seen one."

"Really?" asked Mouse. "Then today we will find a rainbow."

"But it looks like it will rain," said Mongoose.

"That's okay," said Mouse.

Mouse and Mongoose walked up the mountain to find a rainbow. They came to a stream. Mouse stopped by a big rock.

He lifted the rock and peeked under it. “No rainbow here,” he said.

Mongoose peeked under the rock, too. “You are right, Mouse. No rainbow here,” Mongoose said.

“But look, Mongoose,” said Mouse. “The stream is nice and cool.”

“Yes, but there is no rainbow here,” said Mongoose.

On the other side of the stream was a bamboo forest. “Maybe there is a rainbow at the top of the trees,” said Mouse.

Mongoose climbed the tallest tree. But there was no rainbow.

“Bah,” said Mongoose. “There is no rainbow here. And I am scared of heights.”

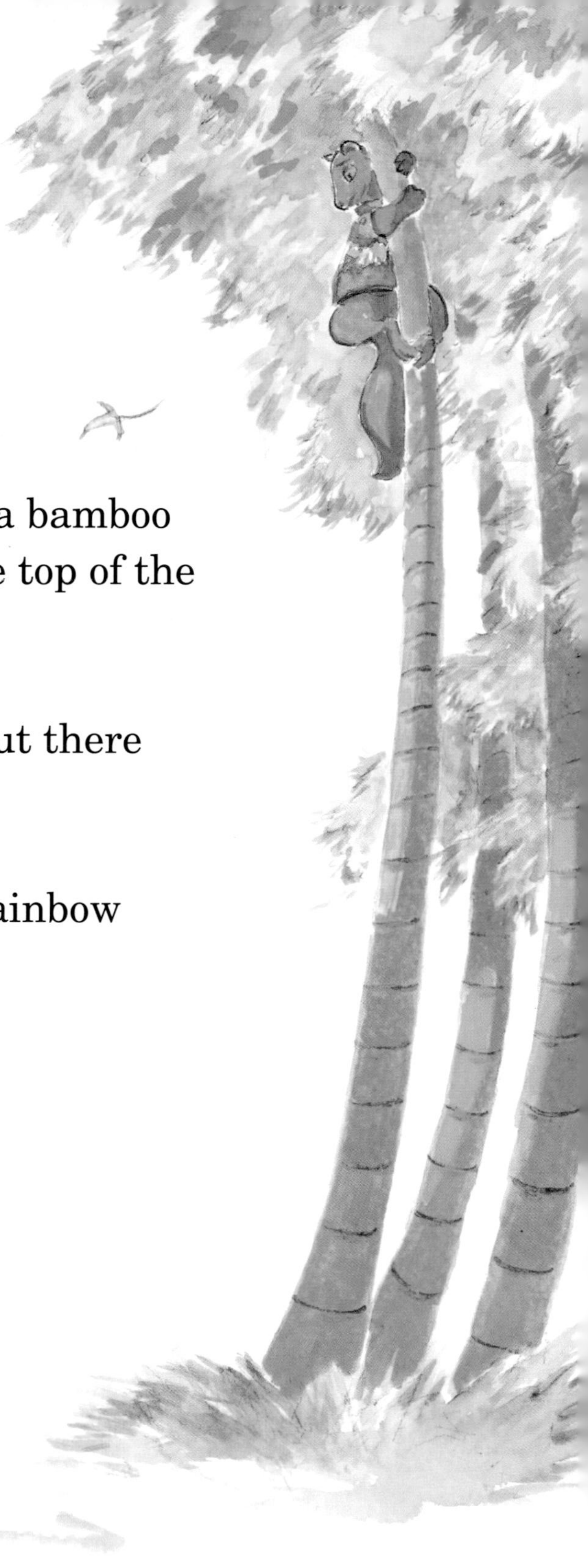

“But listen,” said Mouse. “The wind is rustling the leaves.”

Mongoose slid down the tree and landed with a thump. “Yes,” he said, “but there is no rainbow.”

Soon Mouse and Mongoose reached the top of the mountain. It was cloudy. They sat down to rest. It began to rain.

"I am getting wet," said Mongoose. "I do not see a rainbow, and I am getting wet."

"Yes," said Mouse. "But look at the beautiful view."

Mongoose stood up to leave.

Mouse and Mongoose walked back down the mountain in the rain. They walked to the beach.

Mouse dug his toes in the sand. Mongoose stomped his feet.

"Mouse," said Mongoose. "I do not like the sand. The sand is sticking to my feet."

“But Mongoose, smell the salty air,” Mouse replied.

“Yes, the ocean air is nice, but I do not see a rainbow here,” said Mongoose. “I am going home.”

Mouse and Mongoose walked back to Mongoose's house.

"Mouse. I still have not seen a rainbow. Maybe I will never see a rainbow," said Mongoose.

“Perhaps,” said Mouse.

“But today you felt a cool stream, heard a rustling forest, saw a beautiful view, and smelled the salty ocean.”

"You are right," said Mongoose. "And I was with you."

Mouse smiled and looked out the window.

"Mongoose!" he cried. "Come look out your window!"

Mongoose looked out his window. There he saw a rainbow.

"Wow," said Mongoose. "It was in my window all this time."

"Yes," said Mouse. "It was here all along."

About the Illustrator

Elizabeth Oh studied fine art at the Swain School of Design in Massachusetts, and graduated with a BFA in Art Education from the University of Massachusetts Dartmouth. She has produced scrimshaw, murals, window paintings, and illustrations for various publications. Elizabeth lives in Honolulu with her large cat, Mr. Cuddles, her lovely parrot, Juan, and her husband and muse, Chuck.

Copyright © 2013 by BeachHouse Publishing, LLC
No part of this book may be reproduced in any form or by any electronic or mechanical means, including information storage and retrieval devices or systems, without prior written permission from the publisher, except that brief passages may be quoted for reviews.
All rights reserved

ISBN-10: 1-933067-44-6 / ISBN-13: 978-1-933067-44- 5
Library of Congress Control Number: 2013930619
Text and design by Jane Gillespie
First Printing, April 2013
BeachHouse Publishing, LLC
PO Box 5464 / Kāneʻohe, Hawaiʻi 96744
info@beachhousepublishing.com / www.beachhousepublishing.com
Printed in Korea

Visit our website to learn about our children's book iPhone™ apps, which can be purchased at iTunes™ now!